*For my friend Jane Burns, in honor
of our beloved pets, past and present:
Teddy, Tia, Sam, Dixie, and Truman
—E. B.*

*For Michelle, with love
—Eric*

Henry Holt and Company, *Publishers since 1866*
Henry Holt® is a registered trademark of Macmillan Publishing Group, LLC
175 Fifth Avenue, New York, NY 10010
mackids.com

Library of Congress Cataloging-in-Publication Data is available.
ISBN 978-1-250-10927-9

Our books may be purchased in bulk for promotional, educational, or business use.
Please contact your local bookseller or the Macmillan Corporate and Premium Sales Department
at (800) 221-7945 ext. 5442 or by e-mail at MacmillanSpecialMarkets@macmillan.com.

First edition, 2018 / Designed by Patrick Collins
The illustrations for this book were created in ink and watercolor,
with some bits of pencil here and there. Mostly there.
Printed in China by Toppan Leefung Printing Ltd., Dongguan City, Guangdong Province

1 3 5 7 9 10 8 6 4 2

My Pet Wants a Pet

Elise Broach

illustrated by Eric Barclay

Christy Ottaviano Books
Henry Holt and Company
New York

Once there was a boy who wanted something
to take care of. Something of his very own.

He begged,

and he begged,

and he begged his mother . . .

until—what do you know?

She said YES!

The boy loved his puppy.
He fed him,

and played with him,

and cuddled him in his arms.

The puppy loved his boy.
He licked him,

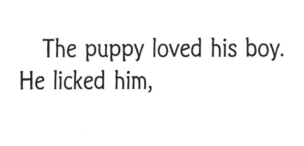

and jumped on him,

and fell asleep in his lap.

They had the best time together,
the boy and his pet.

Such a good time, in fact, that the
puppy decided he, too, wanted a pet.

The boy's mother thought this was a terrible idea. "The puppy is *your* pet!" she said. "He does not need a pet."

But the boy understood that the puppy wanted something to take care of. Something of his very own.

And so the puppy got a kitten, a furry orange kitten.

Truth be told, the boy was surprised at this choice.
"Dogs *chase* cats," he told the puppy.

And the puppy did chase the kitten—but only as a game.
And afterward, he let her eat from his bowl and play
with his ball, and they dozed in the sun, side by side.

In fact, they got along so well and had so
much fun together that it wasn't long before
the kitten herself wanted a pet.

When the boy told his mother this, she looked
at him like he was crazy. "That kitten is the pet
of your pet! She certainly does not need a pet."

But the boy and the puppy understood that
the kitten wanted something to take care of.
Something of her very own.

And so the kitten came home one day
with a bird, a pretty red bird.

Now, once again, this seemed like an odd choice. "Cats *catch* birds," the boy told the kitten. And the kitten did sometimes pounce on the bird—but really it was all in good fun.

The kitten made sure the bird had water and
places to fly and perch, and they got along so
well and did so many marvelous things together
that soon enough, what do you think?

The bird wanted a pet.

"Now, this is getting ridiculous," said the boy's mother. "That bird is the pet of the pet of your pet! She does NOT need a pet."

But the boy knew that she did. She really did.

So the bird brought home a worm, a little green worm.

The boy started to explain that birds *eat* worms, but then he decided to leave well enough alone.

And the bird took such good care of that worm and was so gentle when she carried him and so quick to protect him that before long, guess what?

The worm wanted a pet.

"What?!" cried the boy's mother. "That worm is the pet of the pet of the pet of your pet! He does NOT NEED A PET."

But the boy knew that even a worm might need something to take care of. Something of his very own.

And so the worm found a flea.

It was a tiny brown flea, and it hopped all over the house. Why, the worm had trouble keeping up with it!

But he followed the flea and looked after it, and soon they were the best of friends . . . such good friends, in fact, that in no time at all, can you imagine what happened next?

That's right—the flea wanted a pet.
"Absolutely not," said the boy's mother.
"That flea is the pet of the pet of
the pet of the pet of your pet!"

But that didn't stop the flea.
Because of course he wanted something
to take care of. Something of his very own.

So the flea decided the *puppy* would be his pet.

Oh, life was wonderful! The boy and the puppy and the kitten and the bird and the worm and the flea were as happy as could be, because they all had pets.

But there was someone, a special and important someone, who wasn't happy. She wasn't happy at all.

Now, the boy and the puppy and the kitten
and the bird and the worm and the flea were
a little bit worried.

None of them wanted to give up their pets.
What were they going to do?

The boy thought about this for a long time.

And then he had an idea.

His mother needed something to take care of!
Something of her very own.

Because whenever you take care of something,
that something takes care of you.